DISNEY

LADY AND THE TRAMP

PUPPY LOVE!

Written by ELLE STEPHENS

Based on the screenplay by

ANDREW BUJALSKI and KARI GRANLUND

Produced by BRIGHAM TAYLOR, p.g.a.

Directed by CHARLIE BEAN

DISNEY PRESS

LOS ANGELES • NEW YORK

Printed in the United States of America

First Paperback Edition, January 2020

1 3 5 7 9 10 8 6 4 2

FAC-029261-19347

Library of Congress Control Number: 2019949230

ISBN 978-1-368-05926-8

Visit disneybooks.com

Lady is a puppy. On Christmas
morning, she gets a new home!
Her owners are Jim Dear
and Darling.
It is love at first sight.

Lady's home is very special.
She snuggles with
Jim Dear and Darling.
She goes on walks
and plays fetch every day.

Lady's home is full of love.
She loves Jim Dear and Darling.
She knows they love her, too.

Lady is lucky to have
such a wonderful home.
So are her friends, Trusty and Jock.
They live on her street.

Trusty is a hound.
He used to work as a police dog.
Now he rests in the sun
on his front porch.

Jock is a terrier.
Her owner is an artist.
Jock loves to dress up
and pose for pictures.

Not all dogs are as lucky as Lady.
Tramp is a street dog.
He doesn't have a home.

Tramp sleeps wherever he likes.
He enjoys his freedom
and is always ready to eat.

Tramp makes friends.
He likes to share.

Peg and Bull are Tramp's friends.
They don't have homes.
But they have each other.

Tramp likes his life—unless
the dogcatcher is chasing him!
The dogcatcher tries to take
street dogs to the pound.

One day, the dogcatcher chases
Tramp into Lady's yard.
Lady lets Tramp hide
in her doghouse.

Lady is worried. Things in her
house have been very different.
Tramp knows why.
There is a baby on the way!

When the baby is born,
Jim Dear and Darling don't have
as much time for Lady.
They leave her with Aunt Sarah
for the weekend.

Aunt Sarah is not nice.
When she takes Lady to get
a muzzle, Lady runs away.

Tramp finds Lady. He helps her.
But Lady is still sad. She doesn't
know if she has a home anymore.

Tramp shows Lady the city.
They go on a riverboat ride.
Lady has fun!

Then Tramp takes Lady
to his favorite restaurant.
The owner likes Tramp.
He sets a special table for the dogs.

They share spaghetti
and meatballs.
It is very romantic.
Lady and Tramp fall in love.

After dinner, the dogcatcher
traps Lady!
He takes her to the pound.
Lady is scared.

She meets Peg and Bull.
They tell her she'll
be rescued in no time.
Lady thinks all dogs
should be rescued.

Jim Dear and Darling come
to get Lady.
They are so happy to see her!
Lady realizes how much
they love her.

Lady is happy to be home again.
She meets baby Lulu.
Lady's heart melts!
Lady feels lucky to be her sister.

But Lady misses Tramp.
He comes to see her. He loves her.
She loves him, too.
But she belongs with her family.

Tramp is sad. He leaves,
but then he hears Lady barking.
There is a rat in baby Lulu's room!
Tramp protects Lulu.

But then the dogcatcher
catches Tramp!
Lady and her friends help
him escape.

Jim Dear and Darling see that
Tramp protected Lulu.
They rescue him.
They ask him to be part
of their family.

Tramp loves his new home.
He loves his family.
And he loves Lady.
He knows they love him, too.

Soon Peg and Bull get rescued.
They both have homes
and owners who love them.

Every dog deserves to be rescued.
And every dog deserves
to be loved.